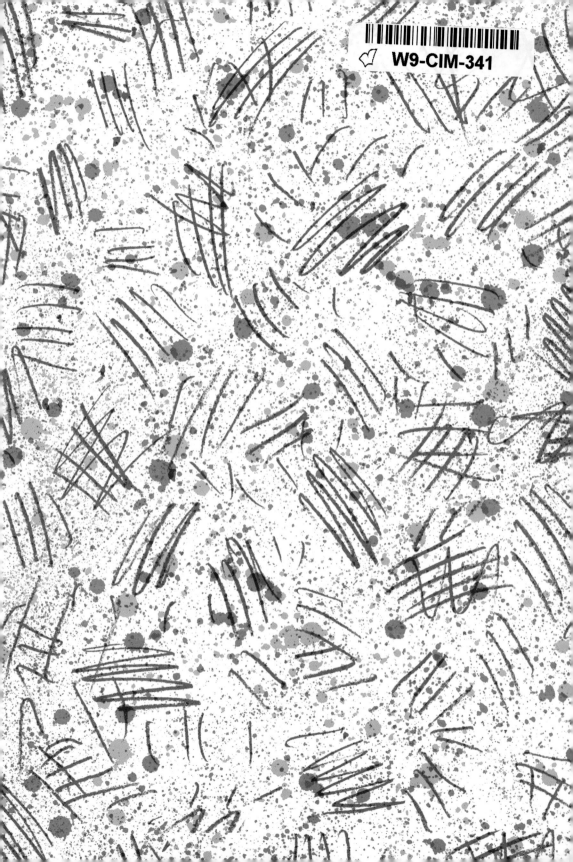

Copyright © 2014 Ethan Long
All rights reserved/CIP data is available.
Published in the United States 2014 by
🍎 Blue Apple Books, 515 Valley Street,
Maplewood, NJ 07040
www.blueapplebooks.com
First Edition 03/14
Printed in China
ISBN: 978-1-60905-366-6

2 4 6 8 10 9 7 5 3 1

Visit Ethan Long at:
www.ethanlong.com

Scribbles and Ink

OUT OF THE
BOX

by
ETHAN LONG

BLUE APPLE

Chapter 1
A SPECIAL DELIVERY

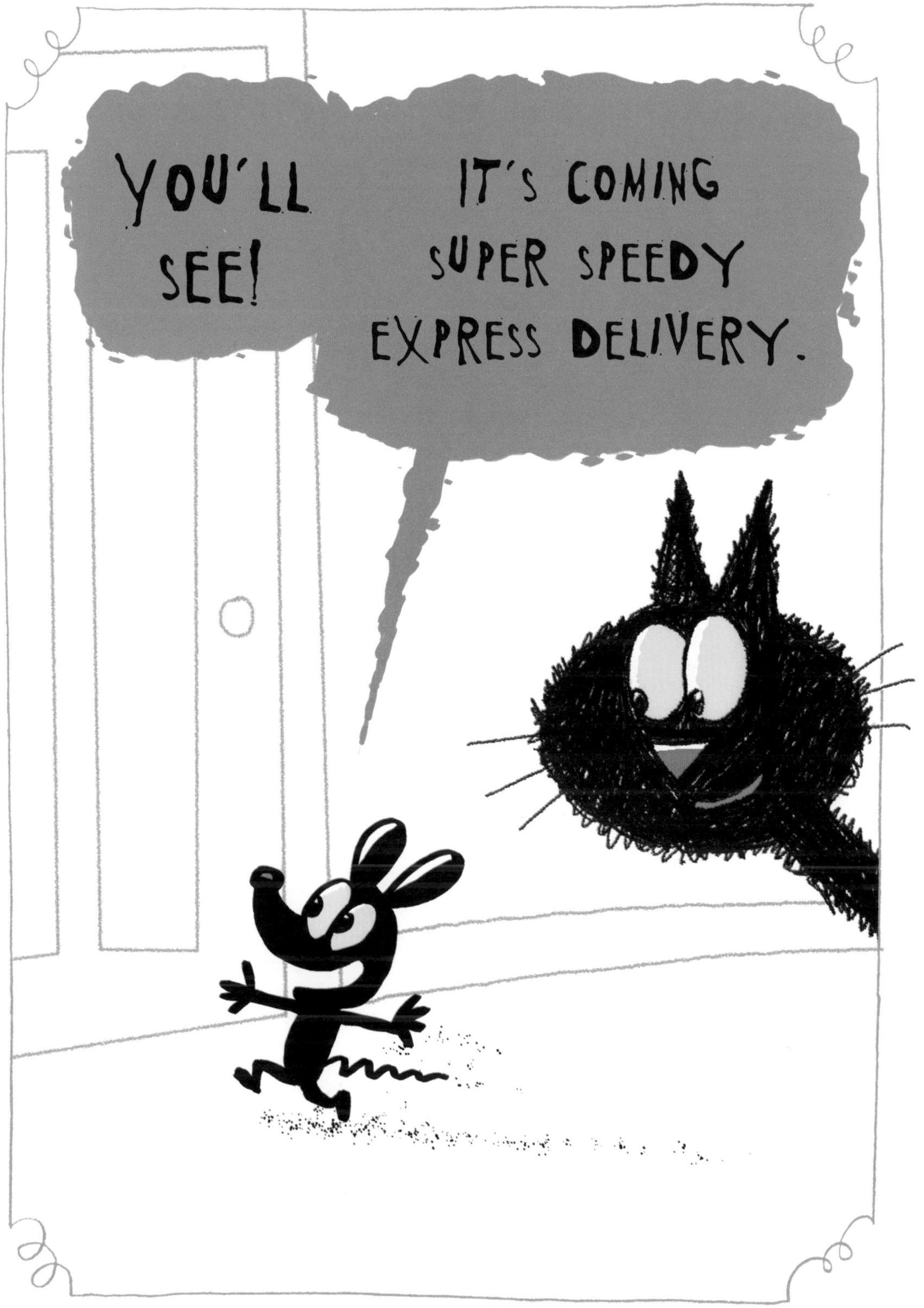
YOU'LL SEE!
IT'S COMING SUPER SPEEDY EXPRESS DELIVERY.

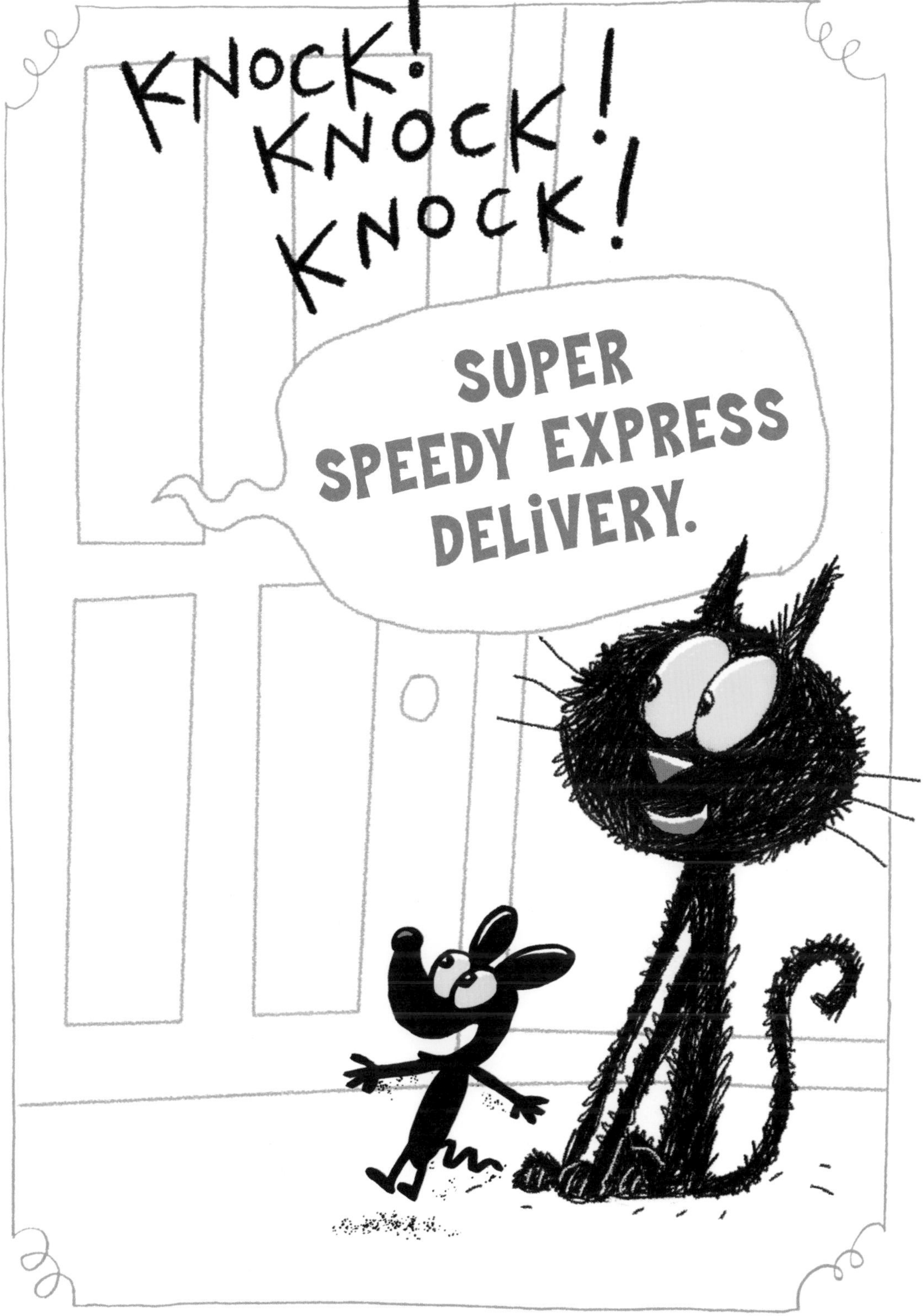
KNOCK! KNOCK! KNOCK!
SUPER SPEEDY EXPRESS DELIVERY.

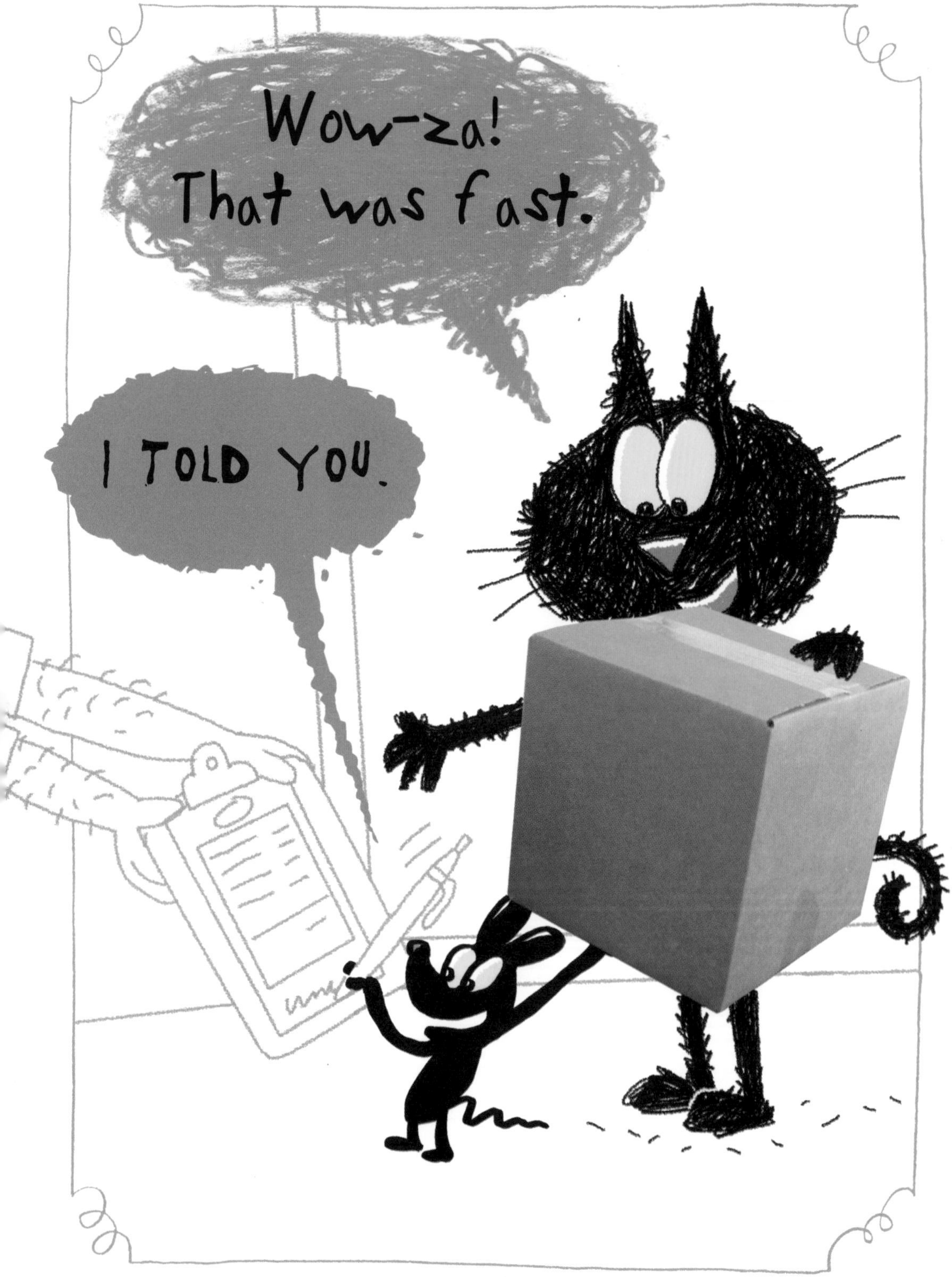
Wow-za! That was fast.
I TOLD YOU.

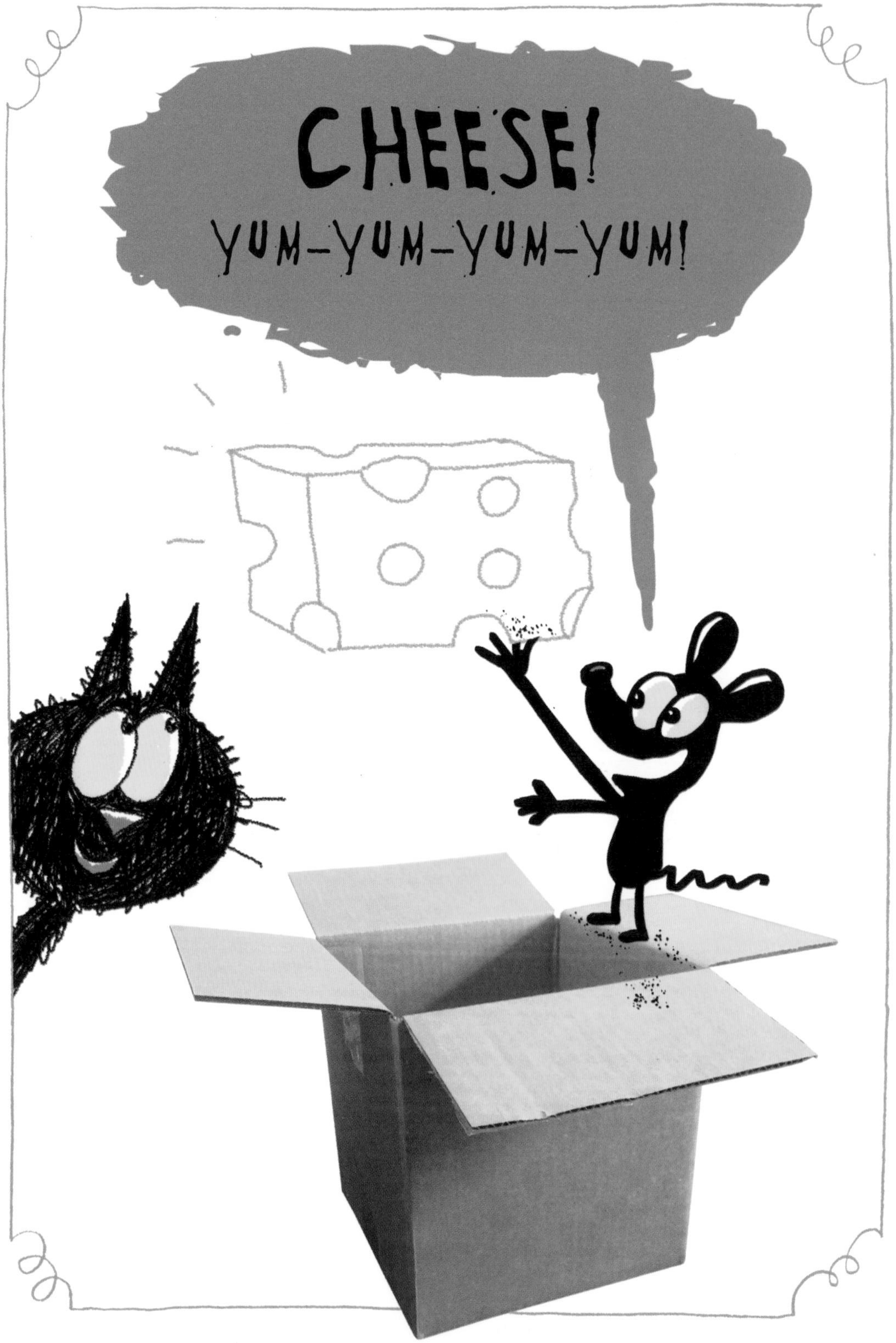
CHEESE!
YUM-YUM-YUM-YUM!

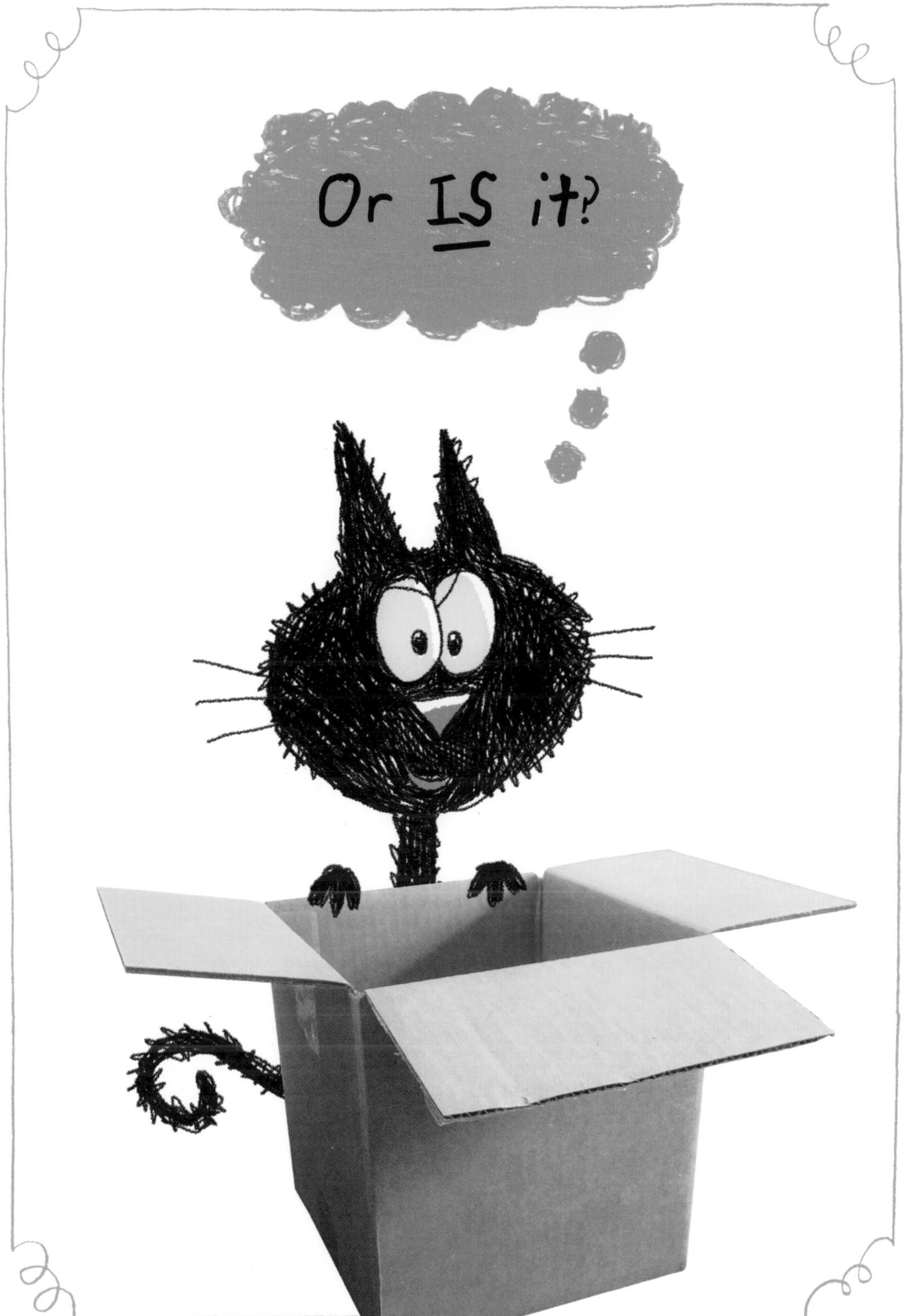
Or IS it?

I love my box!
I love it-love it-love it!

I'm going
to make something
really cool.

How do I look?

HA! THAT'S GREAT!
CAN I WEAR IT?

PLEASE?
PLEASE?
PLEASE?
PLEASE?
PLEASE?
PLEASE?
PLEASE?
PLEASE?
PLEASE?
PLEASE?
PLEASE?
PLEASE?

OKAY! Here.

YOU'RE RIGHT.
IT'S TOO BIG.

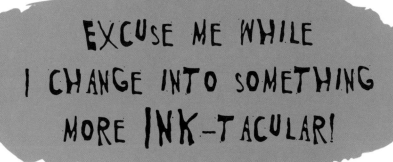

UGH.

AHA!

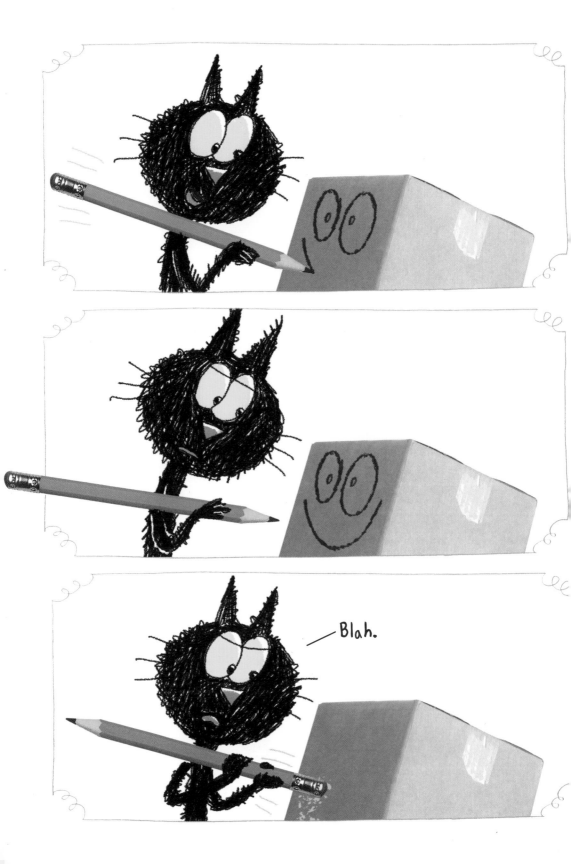

Blah.

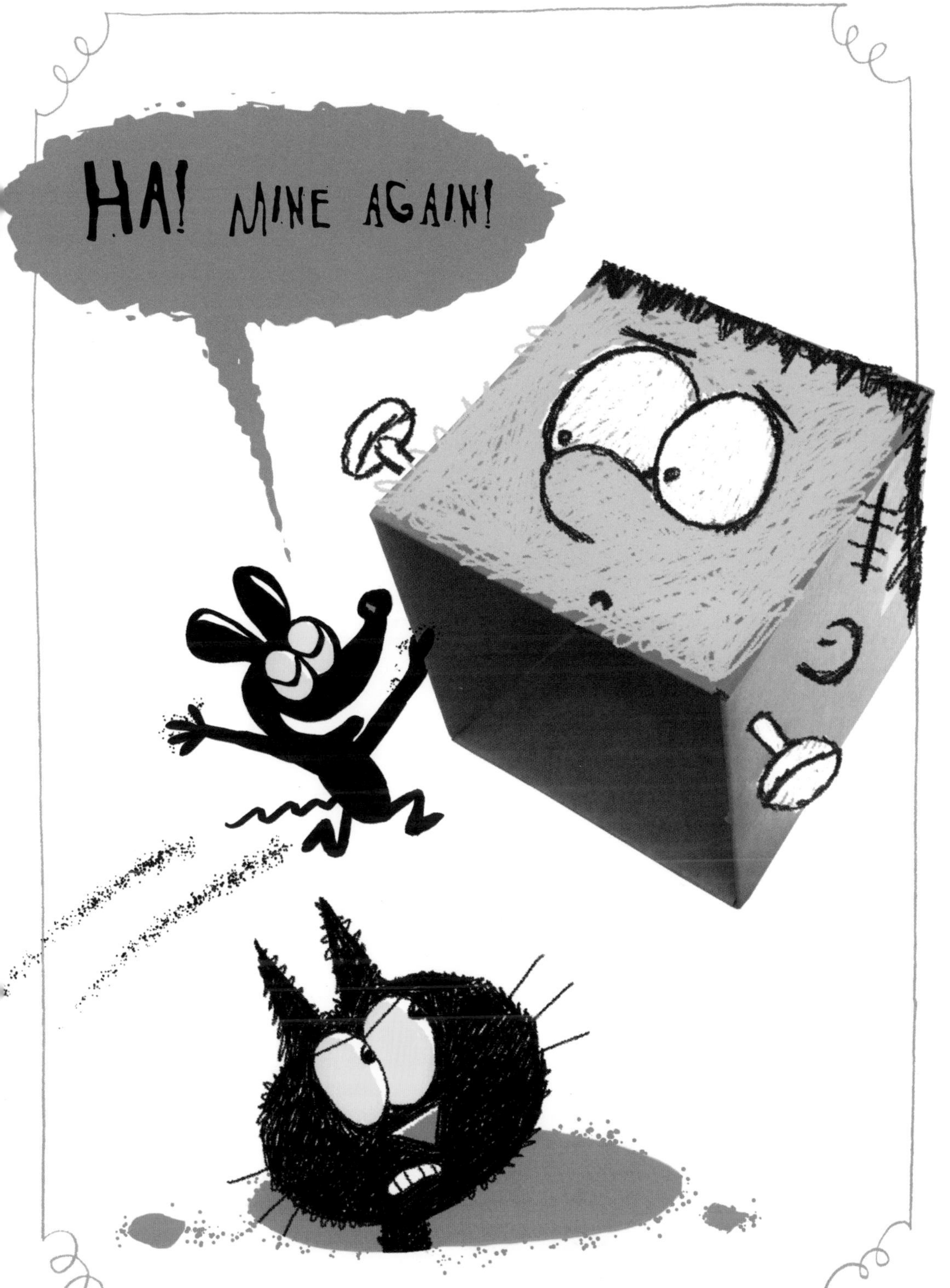
HA! MINE AGAIN!

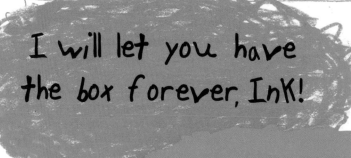

The
BOX
Theater

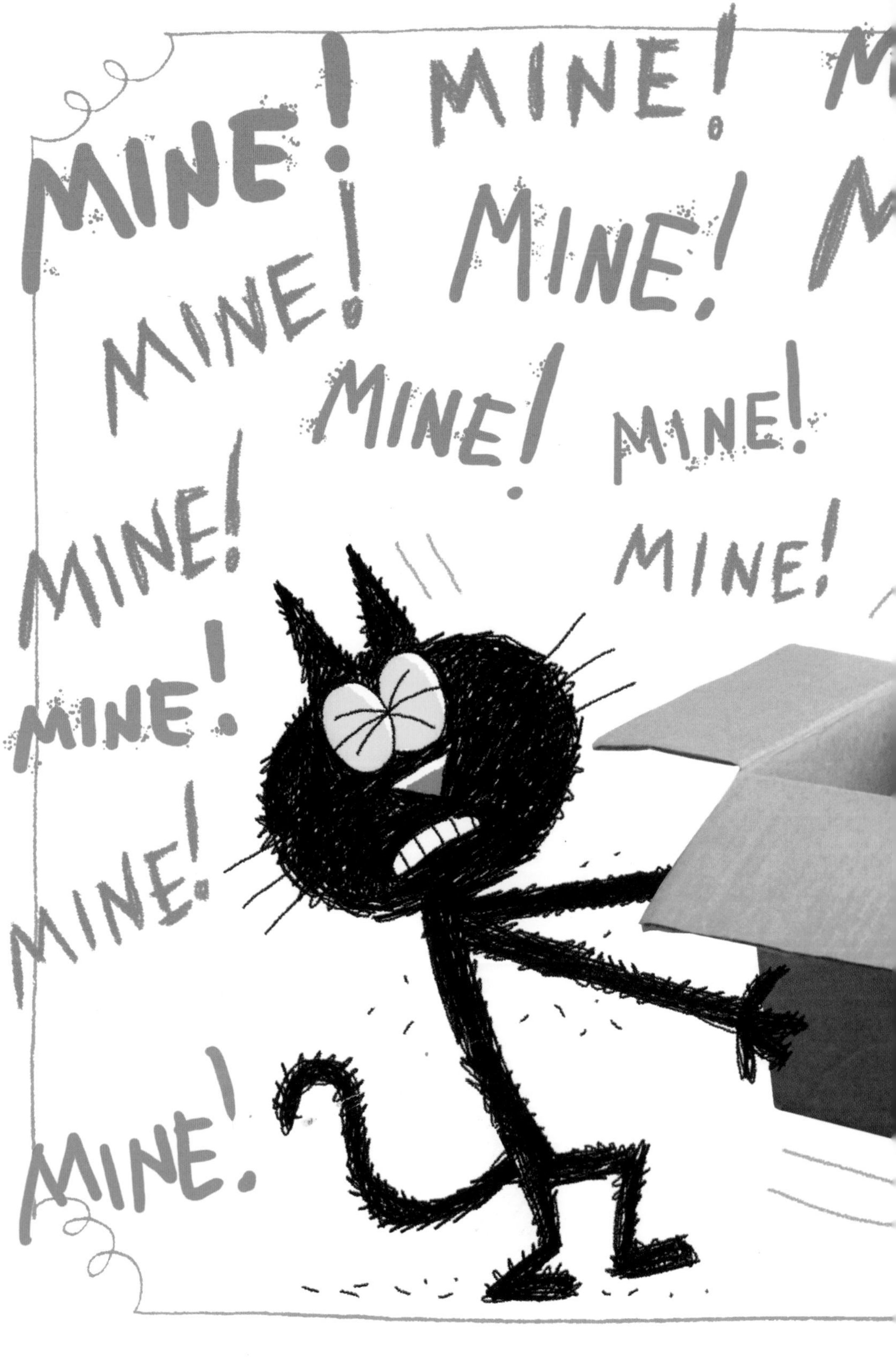
MINE!
MINE!
MINE!
MINE!
MINE!
MINE!
MINE!
MINE!
MINE!
MINE!
MINE!

MINE!
MINE!
MINE!
MINE!
MINE!
MINE!
MINE!
MINE!
MINE!
MINE!
MINE!
MINE!
MINE!

Chapter 4
OUT-BOXED

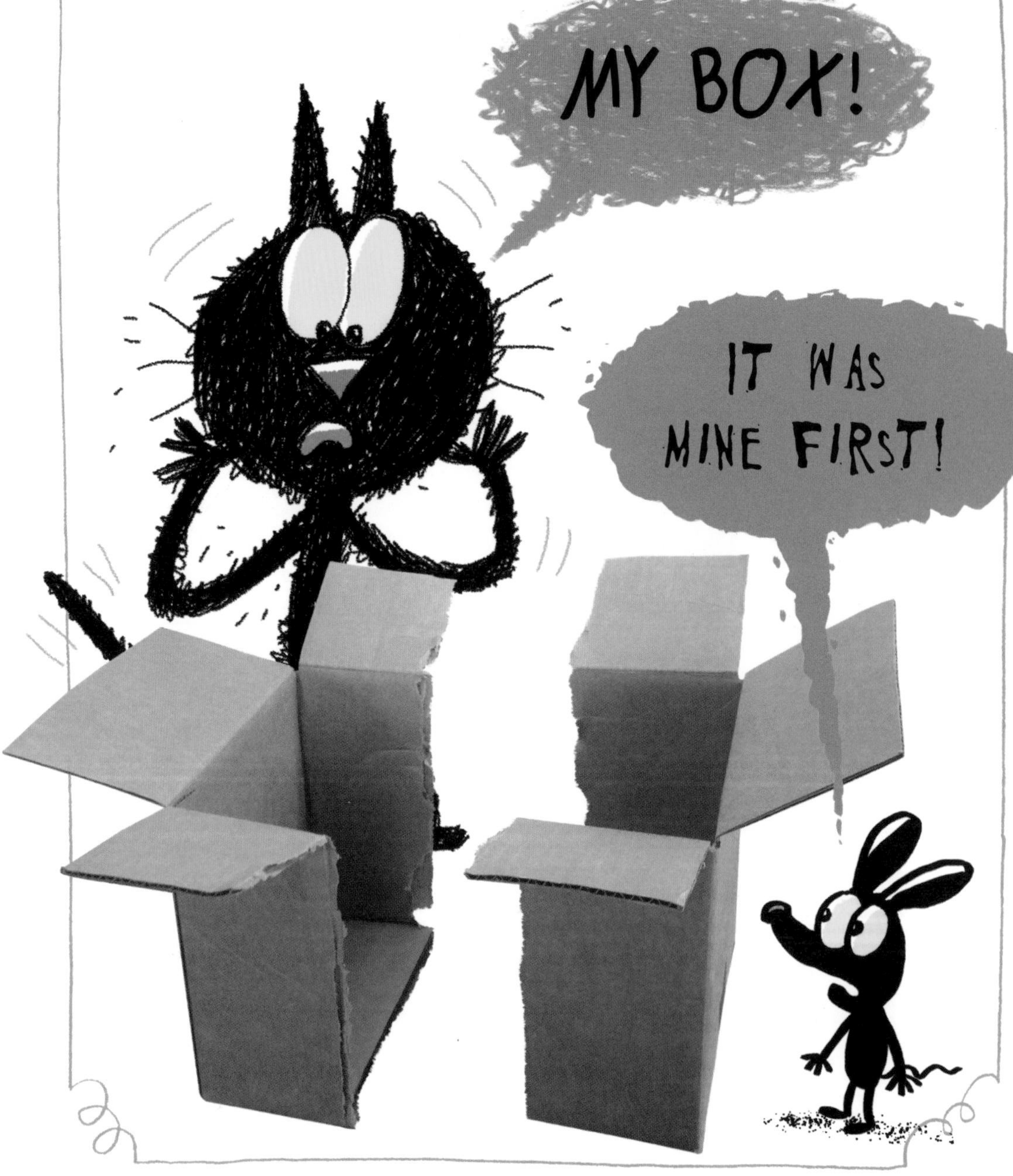

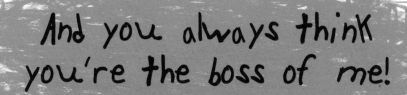

And you always think you're the boss of me!

WELL, THAT'S BECAUSE YOU'RE ALWAYS ACTING SO...

"WHAT SHOULD I DO?"

"CAN YOU TRY IT FIRST?"

"IS THIS OKAY?"

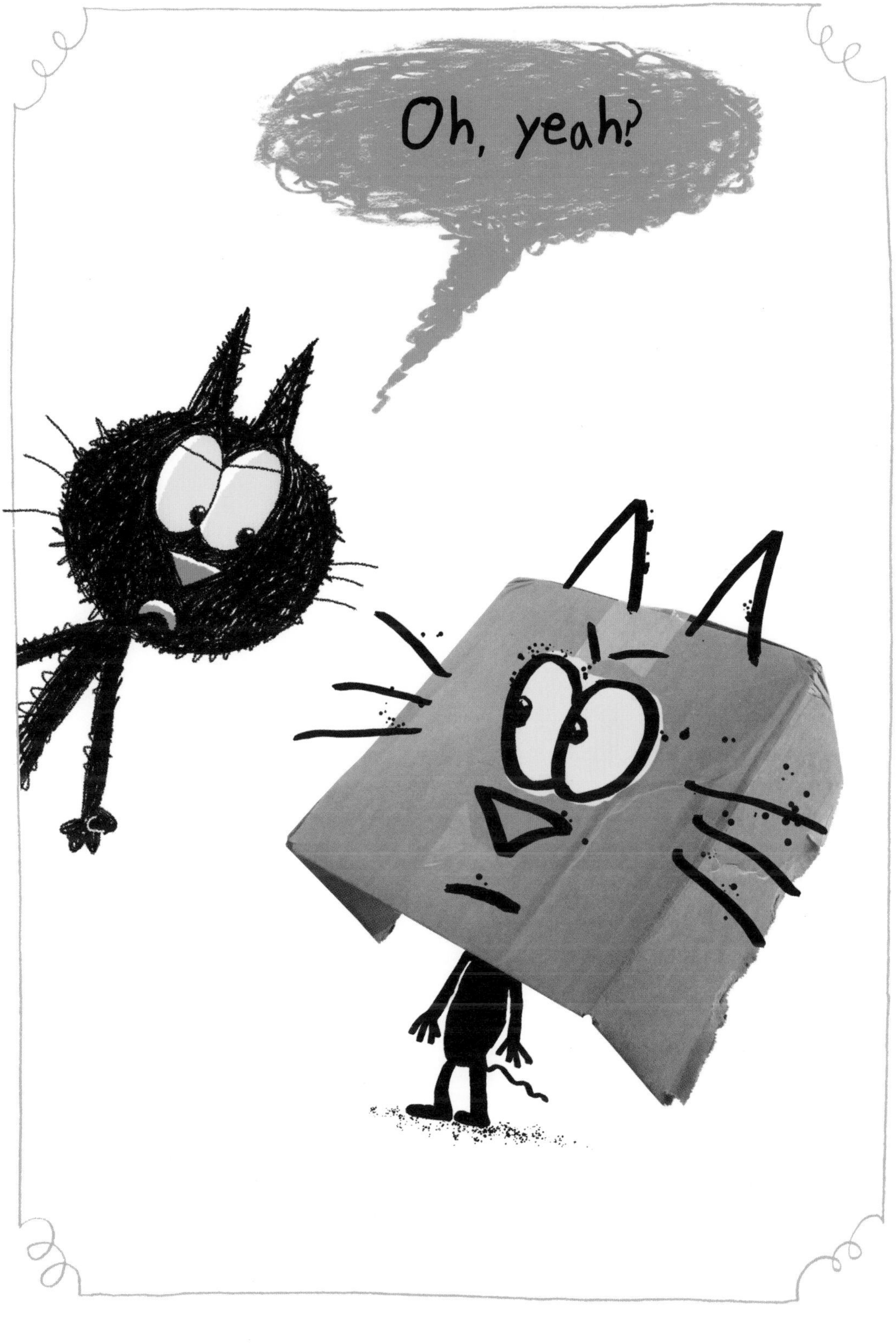
Oh, yeah?

Well... Well...
You're always all...
"Look at me!"
"I'm so great!"
"You're so
STOOOOOPID!"

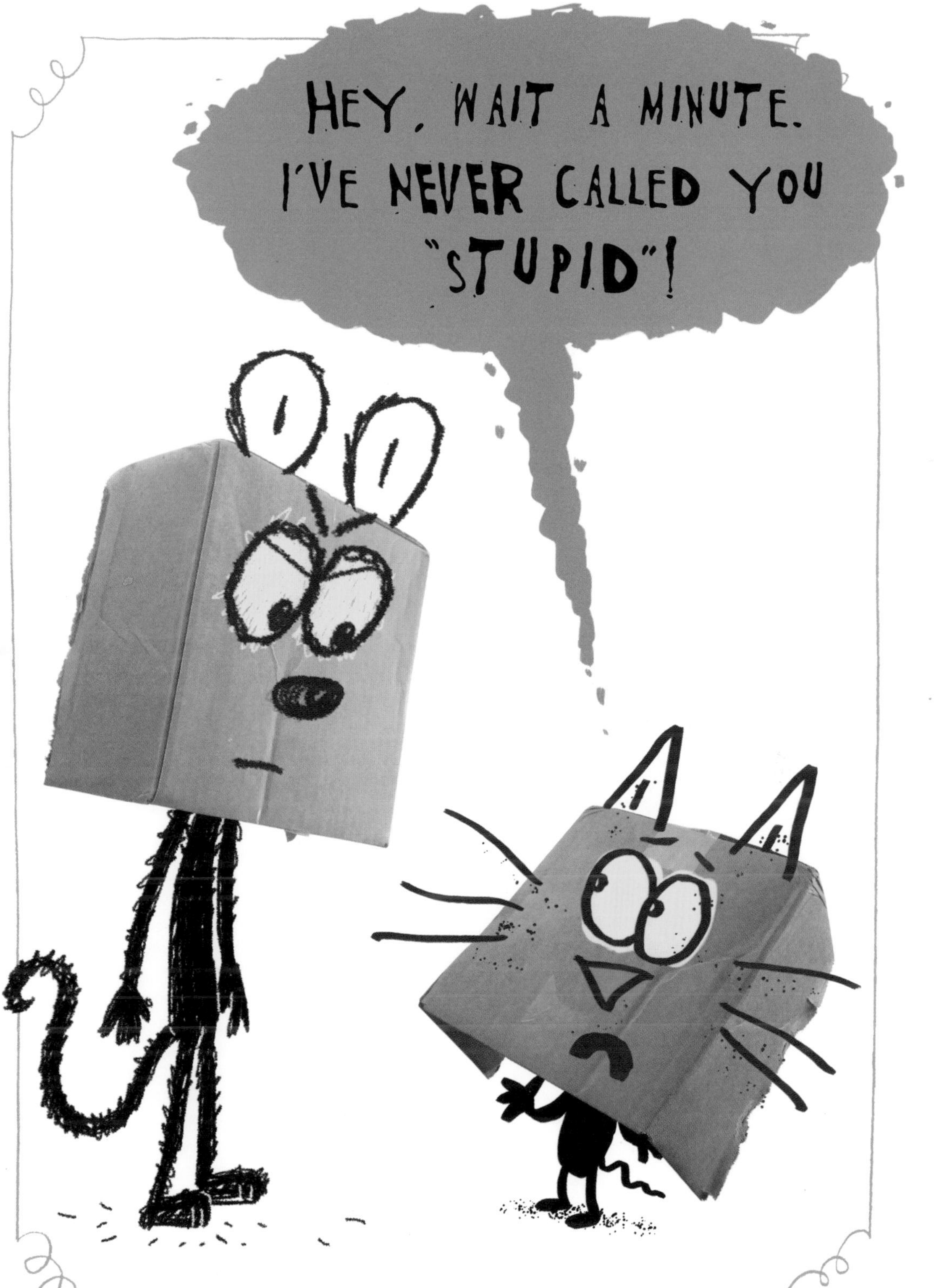
HEY, WAIT A MINUTE. I'VE NEVER CALLED YOU "STUPID"!

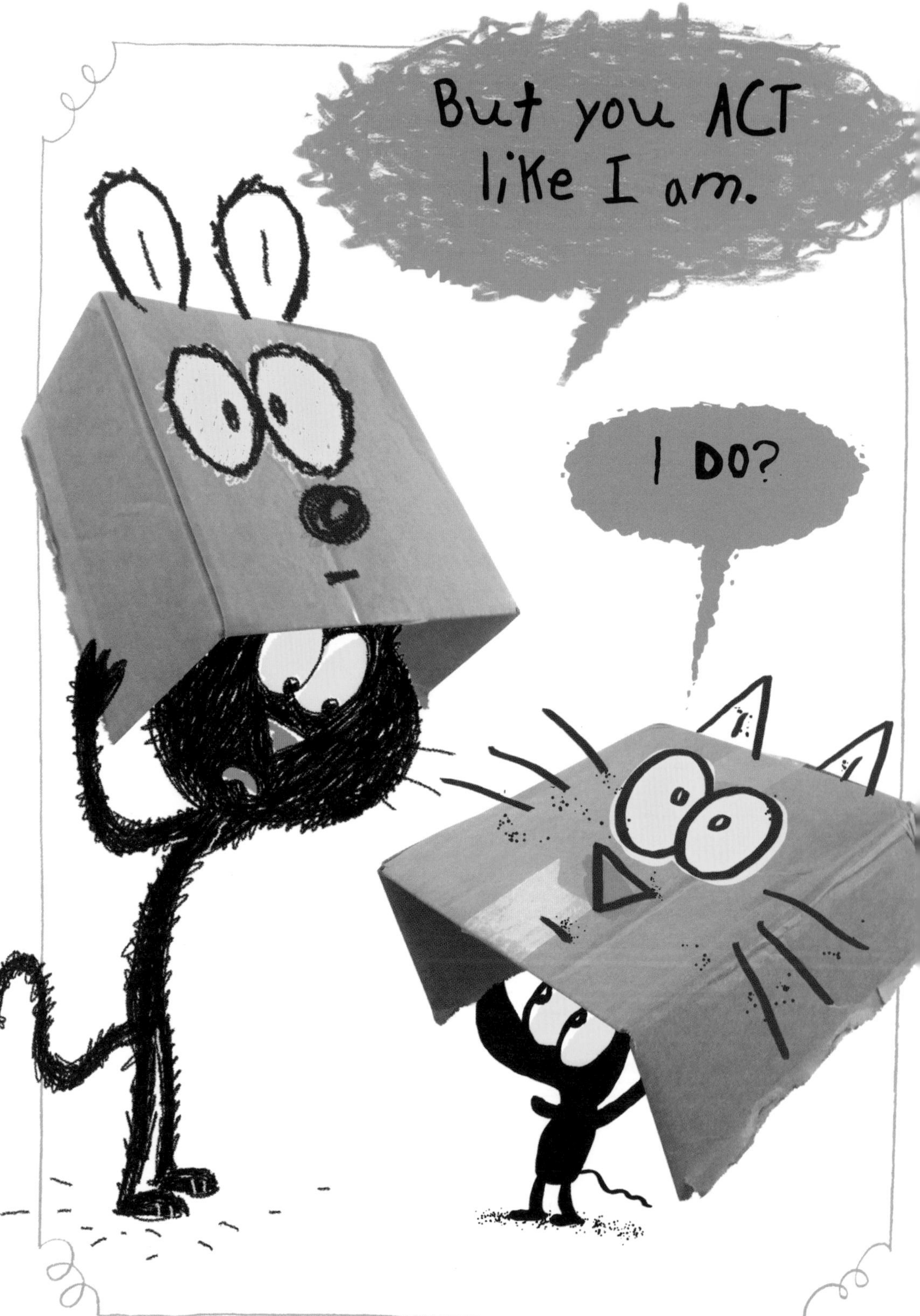
But you ACT like I am.
I DO?

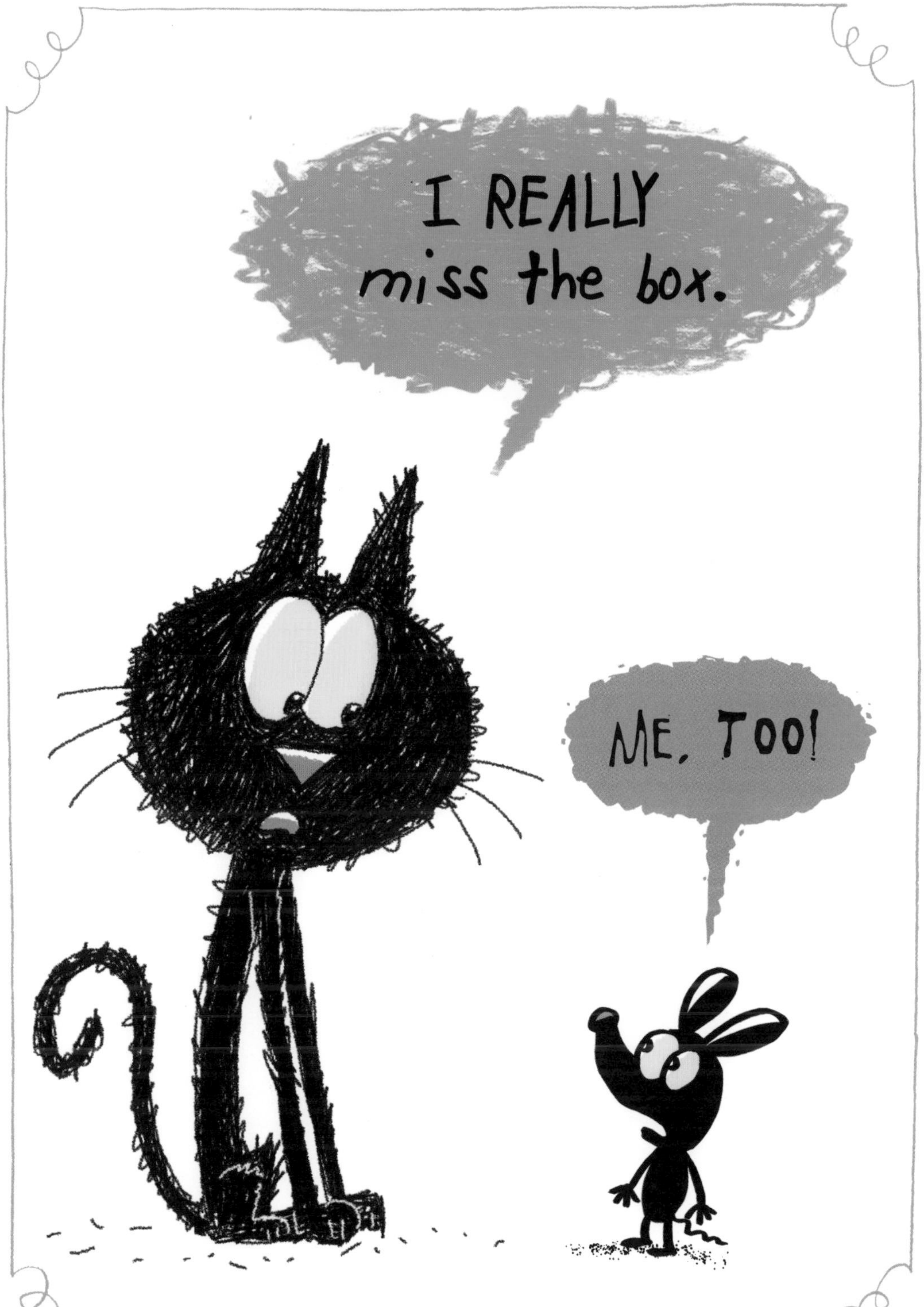
I REALLY miss the box.
ME, TOO!

Chapter 5
OUTSIDE THE BOX

CLICK
CLICK

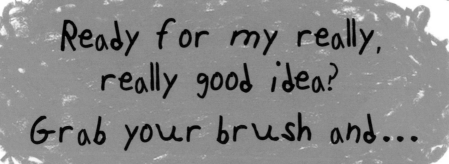

WHAT CAN YOU GET OUT OF A BOX?